Grandpa's Snowman

by Gary Barwin

illustrated by
Kitty Macaulay

D1131598

Annick Press Ltd.
Toronto • New York • Vancouver

We acknowledge the support of the Canada Council for the Arts, the Ontario Arts
Council, and the Government of Canada through the Book Publishing Industry
Development Program (BPIDP) for our publishing activities.

Cataloging in Publication Data

Barwin, Gary
     Grandpa's snowman

ISBN 1-55037-635-7 (bound) ISBN 1-55037-634-9 (pbk.)

I. Macaulay, Kitty. II. Title.

PS8553.A783G72 2000   jC813'.54 C00-930201-8
PZ7.B37Gr 2000

The art in this book was rendered in watercolors.
The text was typeset in Vag Rounded.

Distributed in Canada by: Ltd.
Firefly Books Ltd.
3680 Victoria Park Avenue
Willowdale, ON
M2H 3K1

Published in the U.S.A. by Annick Press (U.S.)

Distributed in the U.S.A. by:
Firefly Books (U.S.) Inc.
P.O. Box 1338
Ellicott Station
Buffalo, NY 14205

Printed and bound in Canada by
Friesens, Altona, Manitoba.

visit us at: **www.annickpress.com**

To the best boy on Bathurst St.
—G.B.

One Upon a time

... when my grandpa was a boy,

he learned to play the violin. He practiced every day,

especially when his mother found his violin!

One night,
snowflakes began to fall.

Next morning, he ran downstairs.

"Have you practiced yet?"

"I have an idea!"

There—a musical snowman!

That night, he played for the snowman.

Many years passed ... and he became a grandpa.

We play together.

We always make a snowman.

A musical snowman.

Grandpa and I are getting older.

He can't come out and play.

"I have an idea!"

"Oh my!"

"Surprise!"